THE ANONYMOUS

I WILL NAME IT SOON.

AARCHI ADVANI SAINI

ISBN 979-888521862-7

Contents

Author

Aarchi Advani Saini.!
    [ ] Author of the book "The Loads Of Poetry"
[ ] Social media "Aarchi Advani"
[ ] Aries, believe in destiny.
    Aarchi was born in India on 25th March 2002, the daughter of Sanjeev Advani Saini(an engineer) and his wife Mamta Saini (a homemaker).
She becomes one of the youngest author of Shamli. So renowned for "The loads of poetry). She has sold the book worldwide, the recipient of numerous prestigious awards in her writing journey. She writes daily columns syndicated throughout the world. Aarchi Advani is well known for her writing on many other platforms. And overthrowing mankind. She is also a fantasy and literary fiction author specializing in "Life".

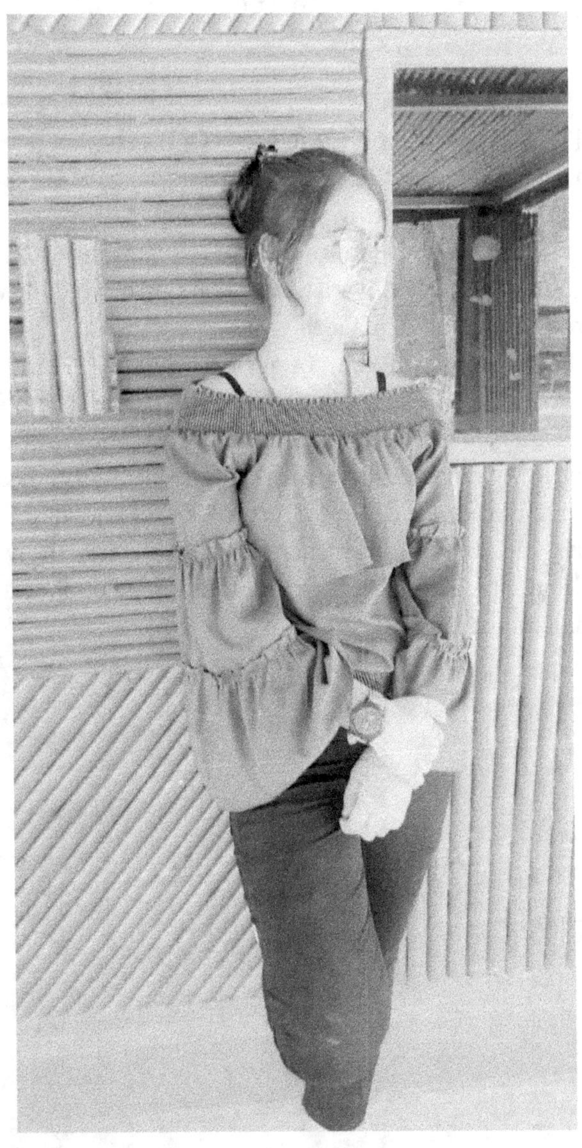

The Aarchi Advani Saini, also hosts a channel where she uses her passion for storytelling. And a background in business to help other creatives navigate their writing. And publishing journey. When she's not writing or tubing she enjoys listening to books,
Making stories on her own. And love to live in her virtual world.

1

"kulhar chai"

Amidst the whispering silences of the late night hour, even the sounds of breath felt like echoing. Kolkata wasn't quiet. Its ecstasy was still hanging out on the streets, the aroma of fish curry was still skipping the casements of kitchens to maunder through the hungry colonies. One could see our involuntary shaking images through the vapours of our hot "kulhar chai", sitting beside the hooghly river, watching the reflections of howrah bridge floating on the river surface as if willing to dive in and search for its pearl of existence. Everything was just perfect.

It was yet another night me and dad walked down barefoot to the river under the bridge with moist soil glued to our toes. Our relation was born to be different. My most soulful companion with whom words were barely needed to serve a medium. My phone speakers created waves of relaxation as they played dad's favourite track- "Ajeeb dastan hai ye, kahan shuru kahan khatam........". But the hollowness created by multiple reflections of strong breeze in my ears overpowered all the voices. There was something today which wasn't perfect.

It took me a while to dissolve each word he said.
"Dad, do you really want me to do this?"
I finally asked him looking straight into his eyes, trying to read words he couldn't say, trying to find even the slightest glimpse of uncertainty. But as always, he was so sure.

"Huhhh......Just go meera. Your mother,......she doesn't deserve such a harsh end of life. I know her soul would be craving to meet you, kiss you on your forehead and ask you how have you been. But she can never gather the courage to say it to you." He said with a piercing quiver in his voice.

Silence.....unbearable silence
For a few moments, no one spoke.
And then he made another attempt.

"Her choice wasn't wrong beta, it was just unfair on our part. And trust me, I've no complaints coz i just wanted her happiness, even if its without me! She is a women of dignity meera, i am sure even today, she would be intensely fighting against her disease just to befool herself that she is strong. But now, she needs you meera."

"SHE NEEDS ME! I needed her dad. The most. I still remember every word she wrote on that letter when she left us, even the smell of that ink, every fold on that paper. How did she believe that her few words of defense could explain sixteen years of my incomplete life! She didn't even look back at me dad! I screamed out Maa-Maa louder and louder but it returned to me unheard. It still echoes in my head. She doesn't deserve us dad. She doesn't."

I felt a strange pain on my left. It was the first time i talked about her and i realised that however i say that she doesn't even breeze through my head but deep down in my heart, she did.

A tired wave approaching the corner slipped the sand beneath my toes, wetted my skin and as dad placed his hand on my shoulder, i melted........don't know why.

"Give her a chance to explain herself meera. Just once" Dad said.

"How can you still love her so much dad!"

He smiled........a painful smile.

"I'll go. But only to prove you that she isn't worthy of your love."

Dad didn't react. I could see him lost somewhere. The breeze today wasn't soothing to him, it just cracked his dried skin of memories.

2

"Portrait"

It's a street enveloped in hollow murmurs and sounds of feet crashing against the floor....the temple bells and the wind chimes...the crunching of newspapers and the polythene bags...the noise of bargaining and the smiles of satisfied customers... perfumes mixed with sweat....and the sweets alongside chaat... Yeah...it's a market outing and we are walking down the slope.

Mumma has some packed deep-fried samosas in her left hand and my index finger in the right...I am jumping jovially as my rabbit-eared sneakers are making chu-chu sounds and my face time n again gets covered with mumma's pastel green dupatta. I have a doll in my right hand. A delightful package!!

A few minutes later, as Mumma makes me walk through narrower & darker avenues, I tighten my grip around her finger, making every effort to stay close...but my defenses fell fragile and the crowd bulldozes over me. I am suddenly standing in midst of these unknown staring faces, scary smiles, and an unsinking feeling that Mumma probably shakes off my hand. I can still see her dupatta getting dissolved at a distance and I have no voice to shout out to her. These demons are walking near and I crush the doll out of fear. The temple bells have slowed down and there's a growing sound of TOONNN TOONNN TOONNN that fades the entire Street and brings me out of the frame.

I woke up to the alarm, frightened....drained in sweat, and looked straight at the portrait on the wall. Eyes as fresh as dew dropping down the leaf and smile as pure as the sound of a flute...This is how Mumma once painted me.

.

.

.

.

.

The floor felt cold to the feet as I walked through the hall. I saw the sunlight perched on the center table, newspaper beside it....but unlike every day.....there was no stain of chai on it.....neither an old song playing on the caravan. Where's dad?

I checked my phone. It read:

"Had to rush early. Breakfast is ready in the kitchen. Don't you go without eating"

I covered my face as I recalled our conversation last night and wondered...was I rude to him? I warned myself not to think much and straightaway go get ready.

____

3

"Prince Ghat"

This city has got some character. It's almost like an aged man in modern attire who holds your hand the very moment you close the house doors behind. It guides you to the yellow taxi, sits beside you, and proudly tells you stories of its history and its people as the taxi reaches the main road. It's a joyful blend of modernity and tradition, of intellect and innocence, of rikshaws and metros, of flurry's hashbrowns and Kusum's rolls, of the noise at Howrah junction and the silence at prince ghat....

I have spent hundreds of hours during my college years sitting in the Indian coffee house, the place where Tagore and Amartya Sen once sat. I have had discussions on literature with random customers at the world's largest second-hand book market just next to the cafe. Kolkata makes me look beyond myself.... My dad taught me this.

As the taxi paused at the signal, a pigeon perched on the rearview mirror, looked at me for seconds, and flew straight

to the massive hoarding of a music concert....
"So that's why the square is so crowded!!" The driver said.
He seemed to have no clue of the singer. But my center
of mass seemed shifted already. The tips of my lips were
stretched maybe....I mean....I smiled perhaps.

"Wait...can he really send me an invite! Well, he can....but....
Oh God! should I even go?" I thought.

An ant of nervousness kept crawling on my skin till the
taxi stopped. As I stepped out...something changed. The air
seemed to squeeze me, sucked all the moisture from the
pores and I froze right in the middle of the street. Standing
two feet away from the glass door of the art gallery....my
reflection was staring at me. Those Kohl-rimmed eyes, mid-
parted hair, a tiny black bindi, silver-plated jhumkas, black
Kurti.....I looked so much like maa! How! Why! It shouldn't
be! I can't see her! I don't wanna go to her baba!

Everything that happened in the past 24 hours rolled before
me like film reels, and I kept staring at myself till the horns
yelled.

"MEERA!"
Rabia broke my chain of thoughts and pulled me by the side
of the street.
"You're okay!"
I suddenly realized that I couldn't afford to succumb to it.
"Yeah" I managed to say.
She didn't seem to be satisfied with the answer and rubbed
my arms gently.
"Okay. You have got some parcels in the cabin...so check
them out. Meanwhile....I m gonna get some tea."

"For me too, Rabia." Tea could be the only savior.

Ritkriti Art Gallery (राग)...stands in Kolkata since past sixty years. Its logo, 'The Sun God' continues to be the most eye catchy piece in the avenue. The passage inside was glowing with slant sunrays and had a set of new portraits installed, I could locate many of my paintings hanged at the outglowing positions. Das babu must have really liked them. I coated a thick layer of pride over all my disturbed feelings. It had been my modus operandi so far....and it worked always. I walked past many collections of sculptures and paintings and as i entered my cabin in the art lane....the breeze changed again. A bouquet radiating a sweet fragrance and an envelope beside it.

It was an invitation to the concert which I anticipated anyway. But what accompanied it was a letter:

" It was beautiful! Perhaps more beautiful than my music itself! I didn't imagine my music portrait as this stunning....which I never should have doubted because you are...you know...you! And neither did I know that you know my music so well that you could paint it!! It so meaningful....
I'll wait for you tonight Rachael. See you!
-Vyom"

Rachael..... my character's name which I played opposite him in a school play.

"He hasn't forgotten it!"

4

"Believe"

Darkness had begun sharpening the curves of the frolicking moon up there and the ambience was in Stark contrast to what I had imagined. The stage was covered in afghan carpets and instruments from classical to modern eras were embellishing it. The portrait that I painted for vyom's band was looking stunning in the spot light and the air conspired with the red lights enveloping us to keep it warm.

"We should've stood closer to the stage yaar Meera" Rabia said irritatingly
"Arey but look the view is much wider from here" I tried to convince her. To which she laughed and said "You know he'll spot you anyway"

Before I could shy properly, the girls next to us screamed so loud that my right ear had an attack. Armouring my ear, I traced the direction of her gaze to the stage. The lights went different already, the floor trembled with a sudden shift in frequency, the ecstasy went a pitch higher and my heart skipped a beat. Vyom Stood there, right at the center stage, glowing in Golden spotlight.

Just like dry leaves rubs against the floor, many voices breezed in symphony...."Wowwww..."
Indeed! Denim blue jeans and black T-shirt with decent in the process muscles peeping from beneath. With laser lights in the bg, he welcomed the crowd in his husky voice and began intertwining the wire of microphone between his fingers as if he don't know what else to do without a guitar. With mysterious low harmonies, he began with his first ever YouTube cover of 'Laal ishq' in his rasp vocal tone and the crowd was captivated already. Vyom always had a relaxed charisma and he is out of his head when he performs. As if he pictures the notes before he hits them and transcends you to the world he resides in.
The concert was an amalgamation of melodies and beats, of covers and originals. The crowd screamed lyrics in unison which he had always dreamt of. He did raise his eyes to me various times and winked once which made me weak on my knees. Albeit, girls in the vicinity felt the wink was directed to them and they screamed louder.

Tickling my upper thighs, the phone beeped and the warmth began burning my skin.
A message confirming the train reservation to Hyderabad tomorrow. The last thing I would want right now. A Strange sense of fright got mixed with my blood and I just wished someone could stop it from happening.

"I am going home" Rabia lingered in the crowd, confused as I left her behind.

I sat hugging my stomach tight at the back seat of taxi....the message flashed on screen.

'I'll be backstage in 5 minutes (Vyom)'

Silencing the storm of emotions within, I let the cold breeze numb my veins. The city nodded in rhythm.

5:30 PM. Next day.

There is something about sunsets and classic melodies together. They make you appreciate what you have. For some reason, I was calm. Tea was waiting to be sipped while I gave a final check to the luggage.

"I....I got your wrist watch fixed. It suits you" Baba said as he slid the watch towards me.

"Is that all you have to say?" I asked with a smile and few pauses.

Baba walked by the window with hands in pocket (Can't leave his swag behind)......still quiet. I had to break the silence.

"Ok look....To me, it still feels like a ripple in our otherwise tranquil Brooke. But you wanted me to go and I am going. Simple. I have my emotional guards on" (Nervous laughter) "And if you are worried about her......she'd be fine." I said while taking the last sip.

"Good that you're sorted in your head at least. Accha Vyom is waiting outside" Baba said while pointing at him from the window. He stood beside his car, folding sleeves of even his half shirt out of habit. His muscles don't allow that easily anymore.

"Why baba?" I exclaimed.

"I know what you need" He smiled.

Vyom hugged me gently and whispered 'Hi' in my ears as he took the luggage from me, a gesture I am gonna remember till the very last detail. The car stereo was playing 'Khidki' and Papon's voice beautifully blended with shades of orange in the sunset sky. The car started as papon hymned 'Mora saiyyan mose bole na' and the breeze hit me to my melting point. I feel lighter when he is beside me, like I don't have to be mature.

"So you haven't learnt driving yet!" He broke my chain of thoughts.
"Yeah, my teacher was busy with his music band."
"I see....taunting Han!" We laughed.
I saw baba diminishing in the rear mirror as we drove through the suburbs.

.

.

Train was about to reach in 20 minutes so we sat on a bench.
"You need anything?" Vyom asked.
"No I am fine."
He dropped his head with a heavy exhale and said...
"You're not. Don't give me that...I know you enough Meera. What's bothering you?"
With elbows pressing against the knees, we sat in the same posture, eyes at the same level, unblinked.
"The fact that she might tell that version of the story where she isn't the villain." I said with a broken voice.
"Or may be that version where baba would be the villain? The man you've lived with all this while!"
Vyom just hit the nail on the head. I almost felt like he decoded me. Intertwining his fingers round mine, he said

coming closer-

"Lets write our version of the story then. They both did mistakes and didn't know how to undo it, they have messed things up. So from here, we can only simplify it. Untangle yourself, create some space for a fresh narrative. What if she's still the women who painted your eyes green in that portrait! It's probably not that difficult."

I just so badly wanted to believe him. He gave me enough warmth to face it alone from here.

____

5

"The End"

On my way from station to her house, I stopped by the nimrah cafe to have Iranian tea with osmania biscuits. Hyderabad has got an old-world charm and its noisy lanes reminds you for how long has it been a melting pot of various civilizations.

On the right bank of the stream was a quiet suburb where I got off the bus, the lane was narrow for it to enter. I was welcomed by the aroma of incense stick as I saw a lady in the corner house, doing evening Pooja before the Tulsi. The house next to it was perhaps the only source of sound in the avenue then. Three girls were practicing sitar in the veranda, 'Ye haseen vaadiyan Ye khula aasmaan', seemingly at the culmination of their training, prodigies indeed. Their master sat on the chair, struggling to spot any glitch in the rendition.

Truth don't scare you in a Melody. Holding its hand, I walked like a custodian of broken pieces, pieces that have forgotten to love but have resolved to learn it again.

I reached her door where a beautiful hand painted

nameplate stood intact under a shade, it read- "Balaji & Kusum Arige." I pressed the door bell without thinking.

Kusum...a name that might have been on my report cards with my surname, but she chose otherwise. For a second, I wished I could wrap myself in the glitter of smiles, just for her to see that she was not an indispensable women. That she left a hole in our lives and we filled it.
But hatred fell in my stomach half way as if someone cut the rope I was using to pull it out.

A small, reticent boy, hair falling over in the front, opened the door and asked me bashfully
"Meera Didi?" I nodded.

He ran towards a room with feathery white curtains. I followed him, so did the melodies of sitar that filled the room like a fragrance. The room looked like a compact hospital and an asthenic, delicate lady laid on the bed. Forehead creased with irregular ridges, deepening as she saw me.

Silence has an obscure voice, it shouts out your inner chaos. She was trying to lift her left hand to extend towards me, failing to gather strength. Tears tried to fall off but got absorbed in the dry skin instantly. She was failing to give proper shape to any expression and that freaked her out. Heavy breath started fogging her oxygen mask, hands began shivering abruptly and an average looking man in a grey khadi kurta came to her rescue.

I? I remained stunned, like a statue at a distance with dust reappearing on the surface. I hated myself for hating her.

Balaji Arige, a man somewhere in his fifties.... Hesitantly sat opposite me on the dinner table while uncovering my plate. It was visibly difficult for him to build a new relationship...or to even strike a conversation with me.

I wasn't expecting dosa in the plate at all. 'Is it a coincidence!' I thought.

"Your baba once told me that you like it. Is it good?" He plucked out cautiously chosen words.

"Yeah. Thankyou."

"I made it after so long. She can't eat it and......its not a nice feeling to eat alone."

"Where's that little boy?"

"Gopi?" His eyes glistened with the mere mention of the name.
"His brother came to take him back home. He is kusum's student. He keeps her entertained by re-painting everything that she taught."
His smile lightened the air the way I couldn't do. I glued my eyes to the plate, figuring out what to say next.

"When the doctors gave their final word, I brought her home." He continued with a painful quiver in his voice. "The ambulance guys asked where to put the bed. I said, in her classroom."

"Where else!" I said as if I knew her. Even strange that.....i really did. How could I deny that it was she who once got me into world inside canvas. It's where I reside today.

His silence caught my attention again. A face personifying hopelessness, but courage still managing to flow through the veins. Out of all that I should have been feeling about a step dad, I felt a pure energy. He was the tranquil surface of a pond, waiting for some boat, some ripple, something to look alive.

"Won't you eat with me.....?" I said while serving him the plate. He clearly wasn't expecting it.

Perhaps I shut his 'Sorry' before it reached up the throat. We then ate quietly, feeling each other's pain. Something was healing us.

I couldn't sleep that night. I spent it with her paintings, trying to find myself in them. Her strokes were magically recuperating me, showing me how beautifully incomplete all of us are. I even went to her room midnight, silently watching him sleeping on the chair beside her bed. They were beaming together in the golden street light coming from the window, just like a masterpiece.

12:30 PM

It was time for the duhur prayer and Azan was clearly audible from the terrace when I climbed up the stairs. Basking in the sunshine, she sat on the folding bed, perplexedly looking at the plants. We quietly sat next to each other for few minutes. I then combed her hair, painted her nails, and moisturized her skin.

She looked at me and said-

"Your skin is so soft."

Pause

"How beautiful you have become!"

She turned her gaze back to the plants. I kept looking at her.

My life was in the right place, in the right shape. I needed no version of no story now. It's good in here, in the present.

The End